Fancy NANCY

Saturday Night Sleepover

Written by
Jane O'Connor

Illustrated by
Robin Preiss Glasser

HARPER
An Imprint of HarperCollinsPublishers

For the brothers O'Connor (Robby and Teddy)
with much love from their mother
—J.O'C.

For my three sisters
—R.P.G.

Fancy Nancy: Saturday Night Sleepover
Text copyright © 2016 by Jane O'Connor
Illustrations copyright © 2016 by Robin Preiss Glasser

Library of Congress Control Number: 2015936057
ISBN 978-0-06-226985-0

Typography by Jeanne L. Hogle
15 16 17 18 19 CG/WOR 10 9 8 7 6 5 4 3 2 1

First Edition

Wait until you hear this! My mom just won a weekend at the Whispering Pines Resort. A resort is like a motel, only way fancier, with tons of outdoor recreation.

"So when do we leave?" I ask. "Should I start packing now?"

"Um ... actually, only Dad gets to come with me," my mom says.

I am flabbergasted—that's fancy for shocked. "But, but, but you and Dad won't have any fun without JoJo and me."

"It's only one night," my mom points out.
Then she makes a call and tells us that my sister
and I will get to sleep over at Mrs. DeVine's.

Oh! That's way better. I adore Mrs. DeVine.
Even if her house isn't a resort, it's by far the
fanciest in the neighborhood.

JoJo is not as reasonable as I am. "No, no, no!" she cries. "Don't go. I'll miss you."

"Let me handle this," I tell my mom.

"I'll be with you the whole time," I explain to my sister. "So you won't get scared or lonely."

JoJo will feel braver if we rehearse for the sleepover. Rehearsing is fancy for practicing. So we go over to Mrs. DeVine's.

In the guest room I pretend to fall asleep. I snore a little to make it seem more real. "Are you really asleep?" JoJo asks. "No," I say. "But see how easy it will be?"

I may not have mentioned this, but I am practically an expert on sleepovers ever since Bree spent the night last Friday.

Back at home, I show JoJo my photo album. "Look at all the fun we had," I say.

Although the real sleepover isn't until next Saturday night, we start packing.

I also make a sleepover survival kit for JoJo. "Here's what's in it, JoJo," I say. I show her the checklist.

Sleepover Checklist

Night-light
because JoJo is scared of the dark ☑

Earmuffs to block out weird noises ☑

JoJo's favorite sandwich since she is a picky eater ☑

Photo so we can kiss Mom and Dad good-night ☑

Voilà!
I've thought of everything!

Before we know it, the big night has arrived.

When my parents leave, JoJo
doesn't shed a single tear.

She even eats all her dinner.

It's chicken à la king, which is fancy and French. I am very proud of my little sister.

It turns out that Mrs. DeVine is also an expert at sleepovers.

We try out different hairstyles.

We put on a fashion show. JoJo and
I are practically dripping with jewelry!

Later we watch a movie. JoJo
falls fast asleep before it ends.

Mrs. DeVine says, "All the merriment has me exhausted too." She means she's wiped out from so much fun.

Mrs. DeVine carries my sister upstairs.

"Sweet dreams," she says once we're
in bed, and she blows us a kiss.

Soon I hear snoring.

"Psst, JoJo," I whisper. "Are you asleep or faking?"
No answer.

It's very dark in here. Too dark.

It couldn't hurt to turn on JoJo's
night-light.

But soon I hear a weird noise, a
scratch-scratch-scratching at the door.
What could it be?

I am very courageous
(that's fancy for brave)
so I open it.

Whew!
It's only Frenchy.

Still, I put on the earmuffs. Now I can't hear a thing.

I can't even hear the clock ticking. But I see it's almost dawn ... that's fancy for sunrise.

I am still wide-awake.

Maybe I'm hungry. My mom says
never go to bed on an empty stomach.

I eat the sandwich I packed for JoJo,
but it doesn't help.

Neither does seeing my parents smiling at me.

"Psst, JoJo," I whisper. "Are you missing
Mom and Dad?"
I am almost 100 percent positive—that's
fancy for sure—that JoJo gives a little nod.

So I curl up in bed with JoJo. I put my arm around her. I can tell my little sister feels much better. "Bonne nuit," I whisper. That's French for good night.

A moment later my eyes start to close.

The next day the Clancys are reunited.
We are all together again.

"JoJo wasn't scared, not with me there,"
I tell my parents.
My dad scoops up both of us. "There is
nothing better than a sister."